MENTAL HEALTH SUPPORT

LIVING WITH
GENDER DYSPHORIA

by Rachel Kehoe

BrightPoint Press

San Diego, CA

Content Consultant: Darryl Hill, PhD, Professor of Psychology, College of Staten Island

LIBRARY OF CONGRESS CATALOGING-IN-PUBLICATION DATA

Names: Kehoe, Rachel, author.
Title: Living with gender dysphoria / by Rachel Kehoe.
Description: San Diego, CA: BrightPoint, [2024] | Series: Mental health support | Includes
    bibliographical references and index. | Audience: Ages 13 | Audience: Grades 7-9
Identifiers: LCCN 2023012509 (print) | LCCN 2023012510 (eBook) | ISBN 9781678206680
    (hardcover) | ISBN 9781678206697 (eBook)
Subjects: LCSH: Gender identity disorders in children--Juvenile literature. | Gender
    identity disorders in adolescence--Juvenile literature. | Gender identity disorders in
    children--Treatment--Juvenile literature. | Gender identity disorders in adolescence--
    Treatment--Juvenile literature.
Classification: LCC RC560.G45 K44 2024 (print) | LCC RC560.G45 (eBook) | DDC
    616.85/800835--dc23/eng/20230411
LC record available at https://lccn.loc.gov/2023012509
LC eBook record available at https://lccn.loc.gov/2023012510

CONTENTS

AT A GLANCE

- Someone who is transgender identifies as a different gender than the one they were assigned at birth. Sometimes, this physical mismatch causes extreme distress. This condition is called gender dysphoria. People can express their gender in many ways. Not all trans people experience dysphoria.

- Social transitioning can involve changing pronouns, names, style, and social activities.

- Testosterone and estrogen are chemical messengers called hormones. They cause sexual characteristics such as facial hair or breasts to develop.

- Medical treatments can help change a person's physical appearance. Young people may decide to take puberty blockers. These medications prevent the release of hormones such as testosterone and estrogen.

- Hormone therapy is another option for people with gender dysphoria. It changes the levels of testosterone and estrogen in the body. It helps a person's body better match their gender identity.

- Gender affirmation surgery can also reduce gender dysphoria. Top surgery and bottom surgery are gender affirmation surgeries.

- Gender-affirming health care is lifesaving. It can improve mental health and lower the risk of suicide.

UNDERSTANDING GENDER DYSPHORIA

Growing up, Jessie wanted to be a figure skater. Her family took her to the ice rink. Jessie was excited. She knew they rented figure skates. She ran up to the counter. But the cashier handed her a pair of hockey skates. "Boys wear these," he said.

Jessie felt hurt and disrespected. But her parents stood up for her. They got the cashier to give Jessie figure skates.

Jessie was assigned male at birth. But she knew she was a girl. She liked to wear dresses and jewelry. Jessie always

Society has expectations for how people of different genders should behave. For example, girls may be expected to like pink and prefer figure skating over hockey.

connected with female characters in books and movies.

Then Jessie reached **puberty**. Her body began to change. Her voice deepened. She started to grow facial hair. These changes made Jessie feel very uncomfortable. She started to feel depressed. She began to experience more situations like the day at the ice rink. Some people refused to see her as a girl. Jessie told her parents she didn't like how her body was changing. Her parents took her to see a doctor.

The doctor gave Jessie puberty blockers. This medicine paused the development of

People with gender dysphoria may feel depressed or anxious about their appearance.

masculine traits. Jessie started **hormone**

therapy when she got older. Hormones are

chemical messengers. Some hormones

influence growth and development. The

hormones Jessie took gave her a more

feminine appearance. She started to
feel more confident. She was happier in
her body.

GENDER IDENTITY

Gender identity is the way people see
themselves. Someone who is nonbinary
does not identify as male or female. A
cisgender person identifies with the sex
they were assigned at birth. A trans person
has a different gender identity than their
assigned sex.

Gender dysphoria occurs when this
mismatch causes distress. Not all trans

Access to gender-affirming health care helps many teens and young people cope with gender dysphoria.

people experience this. Gender dysphoria

can cause other mental health problems.

But there are ways to affirm, or support, a

person's gender identity. Gender-affirming

health care helps with gender dysphoria.

1

WHAT IS GENDER DYSPHORIA?

Gender dysphoria is a feeling of extreme distress. It can occur when someone's appearance does not match their gender identity. It can result when people are not treated in a way that matches their gender identity.

People experience gender dysphoria differently. Some people may have a strong dislike of their sexual features. These features do not match their gender identity. They cause severe discomfort. People with gender dysphoria may want to get rid of these features.

Puberty can be a difficult time for people with gender dysphoria. Their bodies may change in ways that do not match their gender identity.

People can say their pronouns when introducing themselves to someone new.

People with gender dysphoria want to be treated in ways that match their identities.

Symptoms can occur when a trans person is misgendered. Misgendering is when a person is mistaken for a gender that does not match their gender identity. People may use the incorrect pronouns. *She*, *he*, and *they* are examples of pronouns.

Deadnaming can also be harmful. It can worsen dysphoria. A trans person may change their name to match their gender identity. Their deadname is the name they were given at birth. Deadnaming can be **traumatic**. Jason Lambrese works with LGBTQ youth. "The person who they once were is dead," he explains. "But the new person is alive, so their current name should be used."[1]

Trans youth are six times more likely to experience bullying than their cisgender peers.

Gender dysphoria is a mental health condition. People must experience distress about their gender for at least six months. Then they can be diagnosed. People may also have depression or anxiety.

Treating these conditions makes it easier to treat dysphoria.

DISCRIMINATION

Untreated gender dysphoria can lead to poor mental health. A lack of gender-affirming treatment can increase suicide risk. People with gender dysphoria often experience anxiety. These feelings are made worse when people are rejected by friends and families.

Many trans people face **discrimination**. Trans youth are often bullied. They have higher rates of depression than their cis

GENDER-AFFIRMING HEALTH CARE AND MENTAL HEALTH

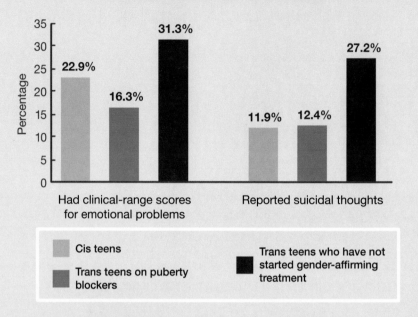

Source: *"Differences in Mental Health Among Dutch Adolescents,"* Adolescent Health, *2020.* *www.sciencenews.org.*

A study published in 2020 showed that receiving gender-affirming health care improved mental health and reduced suicidal thoughts in trans youth.

peers. They also are more likely to think

about suicide. A 2017 study found that

7 percent of cis youth had attempted

suicide in the past year. Thirty-five percent of trans youth had a suicide attempt.

Emma Woodward is a clinical psychologist. She talked about mental health disorders that can occur with gender dysphoria. "We see a lot of anxiety and depression," she says. "It's often affecting every part of their life: in school, in friendships, in family life."[2]

MISINFORMATION

Misinformation also creates difficulties for trans youth. Some people think that children are too young to know they are trans.

Gender specialists disagree. Research shows that children as young as three understand their gender. Diane Ehrensaft researches gender in youth. She says that trans youth are consistent in their identity. "A child will say. . . . Let me wear my dresses. Please call me she." She explains, "That's a child making a clear statement."[3]

People may have incorrect ideas about gender-affirming health care. They may think that it requires surgery. But many trans people do not want surgery. There are other ways to transition, or live as a different gender. Social changes can support gender identity. A trans person can change their pronouns. They may start to wear different clothing.

Some people worry that a trans person may detransition. This means that they stop transitioning. This is rare. And most people who detransition do so because of discrimination.

GENDER IDENTITY VS. SEXUAL ORIENTATION

Sexual orientation is not related to gender identity. *Straight*, *gay*, *lesbian*, and *bisexual* describe sexual orientation. These words describe the gender a person is attracted to. Gender identity is a person's own sense of gender.

2
SOCIAL TRANSITIONING

Some people take medicine when they transition. They may get surgery. Other people may transition only socially. Social transitioning is not medical. It allows trans people to express their gender identity. It includes things like changing pronouns and wearing different clothing. People may begin to use a different restroom. They may switch to a sports team that matches their gender identity. People may try new hobbies. Social transitioning helps with gender dysphoria.

Coming out is one step in social transitioning. This is when a person tells others in their life that they are trans. This can be a difficult process. People learn

Clothing is one way to express gender identity.

to accept their own gender identity. It is a personal journey. Sometimes it is not safe for a person to come out. Others may respond violently.

There is no official guideline for social transitioning. People should make changes they feel comfortable with. A therapist can help people reflect on changes. They can

RESTROOMS

Social transitioning may involve using a different restroom. Some states have laws that allow trans people to use the restroom they feel safest in. As of 2022, there was no federal law that addressed what restroom trans students should have access to.

work together to create a plan that helps with dysphoria.

Children are too young to medically transition. But social transitioning is helpful. Some studies show that early social transitioning has long-term benefits. Matt Goldenberg works at the Seattle Children's Gender Clinic. He said, "Socially transitioning youth are [simply] making the same 'decisions' that cisgender children are making, in that they are seeking clothes, hairstyles, names . . . that reflect their gender identity and the resources in their community."[4]

People may have hobbies that do not match society's expectations of their gender identity.

PRONOUNS AND NAMES

Pronouns are a way to express gender identity. People may use different pronouns as they transition. Some people respond to multiple sets of pronouns. Using the incorrect pronouns can be hurtful. It can be difficult for friends and family to begin using different pronouns. They should correct themselves and apologize. They should not make a big deal about it. These actions can help them make sure their loved one feels respected.

Asking about pronouns is important. People should not assume a person's pronouns based on their appearance. Using the wrong pronouns can worsen gender dysphoria.

Trans people can also change their name. Changing names can feel like a fresh start. "Getting to pick your own name is very powerful," says Anders van Marter.

"It's a way of taking ownership of your own identity."[5]

People in some states can change the gender on their birth certificate. They may also be able to change it on their driver's license. These are ways to affirm gender identity. These changes can help with gender dysphoria.

GENDER-NEUTRAL PRONOUNS

Some people may not identify as male or female. They may identify as nonbinary, genderfluid, or agender. They may use pronouns like *they* and *them*. There are other gender-neutral pronouns. These include *ze/hir* and *xe/xem*.

APPEARANCE

People with gender dysphoria may not like their appearance. They may think their bodies do not match their identity. Social transition can help these feelings. For example, people may wear a wig. They may begin to wear makeup or remove facial hair. A change in style allows them to show their gender identity.

Some people experience dysphoria about sexual features. These include the penis and breasts. There are accessories that help with dysphoria about these body parts. A binder flattens the chest. Packers and gaffs change the appearance of the **genital** area. People should make sure to use these accessories safely. Incorrect usage can cause long-term damage.

BUILDING A SUPPORT NETWORK

A strong support system can help with gender dysphoria. A therapist can help with transition. Friends and family can offer support. Respect makes transition easier. People can help affirm a person's gender.

People can also find support online. The Trevor Project is an organization that supports LGBTQ youth. It offers

Support from family and friends can help someone deal with distress from gender dysphoria.

resources to help trans youth and **allies**.

It has an online community where LGBTQ

people can connect. They can support

one another.

3

HORMONE TREATMENTS

H ormone levels change during puberty. This causes changes in the body. These developments can worsen gender dysphoria.

Testosterone causes the testicles to grow. It also leads to more body hair.

Estrogen is a hormone that influences breast development.

Young people can take puberty blockers. These prevent puberty from happening. They block the effects of testosterone and estrogen. Puberty blockers are usually **prescribed** during the early stages of

The hormone testosterone is responsible for the growth of facial hair and other masculine characteristics.

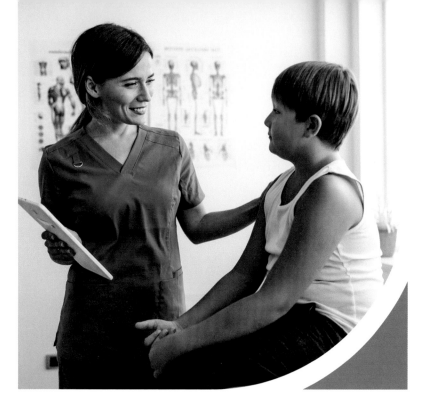

Most people who take puberty blockers begin doing so when they are about ten or eleven, when puberty typically starts.

puberty. A parent or guardian must agree to

let their child take the medicine.

The effects of puberty blockers are

temporary. They can give a person more

time to decide what to do next. A trans

person may want to medically transition.

Or they may decide to let their body develop according to their assigned sex. Puberty blockers can prevent the need for future surgeries. For example, they stop the breasts from developing. A trans man will not need surgery to remove his breasts.

Puberty blockers are given in two ways. Some people receive shots. They must get regular **injections** to maintain the effects. Other people have an implant placed under their skin. It is usually put in the arm.

Delaying puberty can reduce anxiety for people with gender dysphoria. They are less likely to self-harm. Puberty blockers can improve mental health. They can help kids feel more comfortable around others. These drugs have long-term benefits. They can prevent people from having dysphoria about unwanted features.

People may experience side effects from puberty blockers. They may have a headache or feel tired. They may experience changes in mood. Some people lose bone density. But exercise and dietary changes help prevent bone loss.

In general, puberty blockers are safe. "Medications are rarely without side effects," Dr. Jessica Kremen says. She works

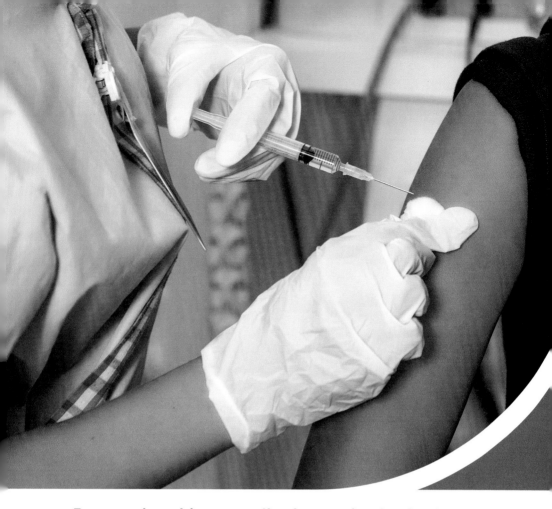

Trans and nonbinary youth who received puberty blockers or hormone treatment had lower risk of depression compared with those who did not.

with trans youth at the Boston Children's

Hospital. "These medications have

enormous benefits for the population that

we care for."[6]

HORMONE THERAPIES

People with gender dysphoria may want to change their bodies. They want their appearance to match their gender identity. Hormone therapy is one way. It is an option for people over the age of eighteen. People who are younger need to have a parent agree to treatment.

Some trans people take hormones throughout their lives. Others may stop taking hormones. Hormone therapy is partially reversible. Some physical changes go away once people stop taking hormones. But breast development and increased body hair cannot be reversed.

It takes time for people to see the effects of hormone therapy. Some characteristics change within a couple of months. A deeper voice is an early development. Other changes take more time. It can take several

TEENS AND HORMONE THERAPY

Specialists study how best to treat gender dysphoria in teens. Guidelines released in 2021 stated that teens needed to experience dysphoria for several years before they could start hormone therapy. Some specialists believe this is necessary. They think these guidelines reduce the risk of detransition. Others disagree. They think earlier access to treatment improves mental health.

years for changes in muscle mass to take full effect.

People who want to have a more masculine appearance take testosterone. This hormone stops people from getting periods. It also reduces the amount of estrogen produced. The voice deepens as a result. People begin to grow more facial and body hair. Their body fat distribution changes over time. They see an increase in muscle.

Testosterone is typically given as an injection. A gel or patch on the skin can also release testosterone. People start by taking

Testosterone is responsible for muscle growth, which is why it is more difficult for people assigned female at birth to gain muscle mass.

a low amount of testosterone. Doctors

increase the amount over time.

Estrogen is given to people to make

them appear more feminine. The hormone

causes the testicles to shrink. It helps

the breasts grow. People who are taking

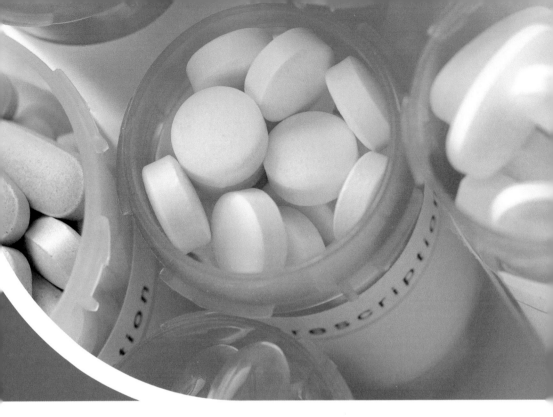

It is important to take hormone pills and other medication only as prescribed.

estrogen lose muscle mass. They also have

less facial and body hair over time.

People can take estrogen in several

ways. It comes as a pill. Estrogen can also

be received as an injection. It can be given

through a patch. People need to take other

medicines before starting estrogen. They take a drug that lowers testosterone levels. They take this medicine for one to two months. Then they can take estrogen.

BENEFITS AND RISKS OF HORMONE THERAPY

Studies show that hormone therapy improves mental health. People report a better quality of life. Starting hormone therapy as a teen can be especially helpful. It can lower the rate of suicidal thoughts. It can also reduce the risk of developing mental health disorders. Adults who

People can talk to their doctors if they have concerns about hormone treatments.

received hormone therapy also had

improved mental health.

But hormone therapy can have side

effects. Doctors may advise against this

treatment because of a person's medical

history. Hormone therapy can cause

changes in blood pressure. It can increase

the risk of blood clots.

Hormone therapy may lead to infertility.

This means a person cannot become

pregnant. People may not be able to have

children even after stopping treatment. They

may ask a doctor to freeze their eggs or

sperm. This saves the eggs and sperm for

future use.

4

GENDER AFFIRMATION SURGERIES

Some people with gender dysphoria get gender affirmation surgery. This permanently changes their appearance. It allows trans and nonbinary people to express their gender identity. These surgeries are available only to adults.

There are several types of gender affirmation surgery. Facial surgery is one option. Top and bottom surgery are also common.

The vast majority of people who get gender affirmation surgery are happy with the results. These surgeries can improve mental health. But all surgeries have

Approximately 25 percent of trans and nonbinary people get gender affirmation surgery.

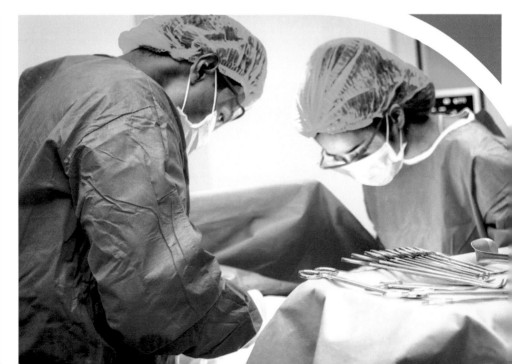

risks. People may experience bleeding or infection. There can be other complications. Some people suffer nerve damage. There may be injury to the urinary tract. This can make it difficult to urinate.

Cost is another factor. Gender affirmation surgeries can be very expensive. Top surgeries can cost up to $10,000. Bottom

FINDING A SURGEON

People should do research before selecting a surgeon. This helps make sure they will be happy with the results. A patient can ask their doctor for a referral. They may ask other people who have had the surgery for advice. They can look at photos of a surgeon's work. They should choose a surgeon who has a lot of experience.

surgeries cost about $25,000. It also

takes time to recover. Recovery times vary

depending on the surgery. Most people

resume normal activities six weeks after

an operation.

FACIAL SURGERIES

Facial surgery can help with gender

dysphoria. These surgeries change the

shape of the face. They help affirm one's

gender. There are many types of facial

surgery. People may get only one surgery.

Or they may get several.

Facial surgery can give a more masculine appearance. Surgeons can insert implants to the cheeks and chin. This creates a sharper jawline. Surgery can also be done to make the nose broader. People may want a flatter brow line. Surgeons can create an Adam's apple.

Other facial surgeries give a feminine appearance. People may get surgery to lift their brow line. They may want a narrower nose. Surgery can be done to reshape the jawline and chin. Surgeons can reduce the size of the Adam's apple.

People may get surgery to change the shape of their jawline and reduce symptoms of gender dysphoria.

Pain and swelling are common during recovery. People may have bruises that last for about a month. Surgeons may put gauze or splints on the surgical area. These can help with swelling. They should be removed only by a doctor.

Doctors meet with patients at checkups to monitor recovery following a surgery.

TOP SURGERIES

Some people experience dysphoria about their chests. They may get top surgery. Breast tissue is removed for a masculine appearance. Surgery can help define the muscles in the chest. The nipples may be moved and made smaller.

The breasts are made larger for a feminine appearance. This can be done by inserting breast implants. Fat can also be added to the chest. Sometimes implants and fat are both used.

It takes about a month to recover from top surgery. People should not lift their arms over their heads during recovery. They also should not carry or move objects that weigh more than 5 pounds (2.3 kg). Top surgery causes scarring. Not following these instructions can cause difficulties with healing. It can cause scars to stretch and become bigger.

BOTTOM SURGERIES

Bottom surgery affects the genital region. This area may be a source of distress. A trans man may get bottom surgery to construct a penis. Surgery can remove female parts.

A trans woman may have her testicles removed. She may also choose to get a surgery that creates a vagina. Skin from the penis is used to make the vagina.

People remain in the hospital for three to six days after bottom surgery. They should avoid high levels of physical activity for about six weeks. People may need to use a

Patients will need to rest and avoid difficult activity in the weeks after getting bottom surgery.

catheter after some bottom surgeries. This

device helps them urinate during recovery.

LIFE AFTER TRANSITION

Some states have introduced bills to limit

access to health care for trans youth. Health

insurance plans do not always cover gender

affirmation surgery. But gender-affirming

health care is lifesaving. It can improve mental health. It reduces the risk of suicide. It is medically necessary.

Approximately 300,000 US teens identified as trans in 2022. Most people who experience dysphoria first have symptoms in childhood. Living with gender dysphoria is difficult. Social transitioning and gender-affirming health care help.

GENDER EUPHORIA

Gender euphoria is a feeling of joy. It is when a person's body matches their gender identity. People feel confident. They have improved mental health. Gender-affirming health care can help people achieve gender euphoria.

Ada Powers is a trans woman. She shared her experience with transitioning. "Nothing feels more exciting, scary, and wonderful than deciding to really move into yourself," she said. "I like people to know just how much happiness was waiting for me after my transition."[7]

GLOSSARY

allies

people who support LGBTQ people but are not LGBTQ themselves

discrimination

unfair treatment of people based on some aspect of their identity, such as gender

genital

relating to the sexual organs

injections

shots or medication given through the skin

prescribed

formally given as a medicine

puberty

a developmental period during which the reproductive system matures

symptoms

signs of a condition or disease

traumatic

extremely stressful

SOURCE NOTES

CHAPTER ONE: WHAT IS GENDER DYSPHORIA?

1. Quoted in "Why Deadnaming Is Harmful," *Cleveland Clinic*, November 18, 2021. https://health.clevelandclinic.org.

2. Quoted in Caroline Miller, "Transgender Kids and Gender Dysphoria," *Child Mind Institute*, February 2, 2023. https://childmind.org.

3. Quoted in Jon Brooks, "Is Three Too Young for Children to Know They're a Different Gender? Transgender Researchers Disagree," *KQED*, August 26, 2018. www.kqed.org.

CHAPTER TWO: SOCIAL TRANSITIONING

4. Quoted in Alan Mozes, "Most Transgender Children Stick with Gender Identity Five Years Later: Study," *US News*, May 4, 2022. www.usnews.com.

5. Quoted in Dan Stahl, "Making a Name for Yourself: For Trans People, It's 'Life-Changing,'" *NBC News*, September 6, 2019. www.nbcnews.com.

CHAPTER THREE: HORMONE TREATMENTS

6. Quoted in Lena Wilson, "What Are Puberty Blockers?" *New York Times*, May 11, 2021. www.nytimes.com.

CHAPTER FOUR: GENDER AFFIRMATION SURGERIES

7. Quoted in Marceline Cook, "Ten Transgender People Share What They Wish They Knew Before Transitioning," *Self*, August 29, 2017. www.self.com.

FOR FURTHER RESEARCH

BOOKS

Juno Dawson, *What's the T?* Naperville, IL: Sourcebooks Fire, 2022.

Tammy Gagne, *Understanding Gender Dysphoria*. San Diego, CA: BrightPoint Press, 2022.

Rebecca Stanborough, *She/He/They/Them: Understanding Gender Identity.* Minneapolis, MN: Capstone Publishing, 2020.

INTERNET SOURCES

Emily Bazelon, "The Battle over Gender Therapy," *New York Times*, June 15, 2022. www.nytimes.com.

Jon Brooks, "Is Three Too Young for Children to Know They're a Different Gender? Transgender Researchers Disagree," *KQED*, August 26, 2018. www.kqed.org.

Caroline Miller, "Transgender Kids and Gender Dysphoria," *Child Mind Institute*, November 7, 2022. https://childmind.org.

WEBSITES

GLAAD: Transgender Resources
www.glaad.org/transgender/resources

GLAAD works to promote LGBTQ voices and stories. It also has resources and information for trans people.

National Center for Transgender Equality
https://transequality.org

The National Center for Transgender Equality was founded by trans activists in 2003. The organization works to amplify trans voices and support policies and laws that promote equality for all genders.

The Trevor Project
www.thetrevorproject.org

The Trevor Project is the world's largest LGBTQ suicide prevention and crisis management organization.

INDEX

IMAGE CREDITS

ABOUT THE AUTHOR

Rachel Kehoe is writer and children's author from Burlington, Ontario. She has written for *Muse*, *Faces*, and *Science News for Students*. Rachel has also published several educational books for children on science, technology, climate change, and mental health awareness.